AF206992

Safe Travels for Squirrels

by Maxime Bonneau with Joanne Mattern

RED CHAIR PRESS

Egremont, Massachusetts

Red Chair Press
BOOKS FOR YOUNG READERS

Wildlife Rescue is produced and published by Red Chair Press:

Red Chair Press LLC   PO Box 333   South Egremont, MA 01258-0333
www.redchairpress.com

Publisher's Cataloging-In-Publication Data
Names: Bonneau, Maxime, author. | Mattern, Joanne, 1963- author.
Title: Safe travels for squirrels / by Maxime Bonneau and Joanne Mattern.

Description: South Egremont, MA : Red Chair Press, [2022] | Series:
    Wildlife rescue | Interest age level: 007-010. | Includes index and
    suggested resources for further reading. | Summary: "This series looks
    at unusual ways people around the world have come to the rescue of
    endangered species by providing safe ways to adapt to their changing
    habitats. Forest villages in France, England, the U.S. and Australia
    feature rope bridges and buckets of acorns for squirrels. Readers will
    meet some of the rescuers helping these little red squirrels survive"
    --Provided by publisher.

Identifiers: ISBN 9781643711881 (hardcover) | ISBN 9781643711928
    (softcover) | ISBN 9781643711966 (ePDF) | ISBN 9781643712000 (ePub 3
    S&L) | ISBN 9781643712048 (ePub 3 TR) | ISBN 9781643712086 (Kindle)

Subjects: LCSH: Wildlife habitat improvement--Juvenile literature. |
    Wildlife rescue--Juvenile literature. | Animals and civilization--
    Juvenile literature. | Squirrels--Conservation--Juvenile literature. |
    CYAC: Wildlife habitat improvement. | Wildlife rescue. | Animals and
    civilization. | Squirrels.

Classification: LCC SK356.W54 B66 2022 (print) | LCC SK356.W54 (ebook) |
    DDC 333.95/416--dc23

LC record available at: https://lccn.loc.gov/2021945554

Photo credits: Cover, p. 6, 8, 12–23, 27: Maxime Bonneau; p. 1, 4, 5, 6, 7, 9, 10, 11,
15, back cover: iStock; p. 24, 25, 26: Shutterstock

Printed in United States of America
0422 1P CGF22

Table of Contents

Meet the Red Squirrel

The red squirrel lives all over Europe. It's easy to spot one of these little creatures. They have red fur and a long red tail. Its tail helps the squirrel balance as it walks and jumps.

FAST FACTS:

The red squirrel weighs about 350 grams, just under one pound.

Their average life span is 5 to 7 years. Adults are seen with hair called brushes above their ears.

Red squirrels are small, but they are good athletes. These little creatures can really climb. They jump from tree to tree. Sometimes you will see a red squirrel stretching on a tree trunk. It hangs on with its back legs and stretches its body and front legs. Like an athlete, this stretching helps the squirrel to run and jump more easily.

Like an athlete, the red squirrel stretches its legs.

Red squirrels have long tufts of
hair called brushes on their ears.

Red squirrels live in trees. They travel through the trees and fields to find food. Hazelnuts are this squirrel's favorite food. They also eat nuts from other trees. The red squirrel also sleeps several times each day. It looks for a safe place in the fork of a tree. It naps 15 to 30 minutes with one eye open to watch for danger.

Traffic Danger!

Squirrels face danger on the ground. In the past, there was plenty of open space for squirrels to run. Today, there are many busy roads there instead. Squirrels don't know to look both ways before crossing the road. Sadly, many squirrels are hit and killed by cars. Because of this, the European red squirrel may soon be **extinct** in Great Britain. The animal is also in serious danger in France since 1950 as its population goes down rapidly.

A Special Plan

The people of Villevaudé, France, felt bad about the squirrels. In 2010, Dominique Baillie started a group called SOS Red Squirrels and Wildlife. Dominique decided to build a special bridge to help the squirrels cross the highway.

Dominique (left) and members of the SOS Group meet regularly to improve and repair their rope bridges.

SOS Écureuil Roux & Espèces Sauvages
Détail de l'écuroduc raccordé aux 2 fusibles
SOS Écureuil Roux & Espèces Sauvages
Détail de la partie émerillon raccordé au palan
Détail des parties fusibles raccordées à l'émerillon et à l'écuroduc
Astuce de prétention du palan
Afin de faciliter le montage du Leaf, il
faudra mettre l'écuroduc en prétention:
- Mettre une sangle autour du pied de
l'arbre (rouge sur la photo),
- Mettre un nœud de prussik sur le cordage
du palan et le raccorder au mousqueton
sur la sangle,
- Tendre le palan la main et reprendre le
mou au nœud de prussik.

Dominique and his friends studied the best way to build their bridge. They decided to stretch a rope between two trees on either side of the road. The squirrels could use this bridge instead of walking on the highway.

Building the Bridge

Building the squirrel bridge took a lot of planning. The rope had to be **anchored** to the trees. The rope had to be strong enough to hold the squirrels. It also had to be strong enough to stay up during storms.

The work can be very difficult swinging from ropes and often working upside down!

Putting the ropes in the trees is difficult work.

Zoé and Stéphane are expert climbers who help the SOS Group install ropes.

A group that climbs mountains **donated** thick, heavy ropes. A man named Laurent Sulfour installed the rope. Laurent used chains and **pulleys** to keep the rope tight. The workers also made sure the tree was not damaged by anything they put up.

Tasty Treats

The SOS Group knew that food is the best way to train the squirrels to use the bridge. Every morning, a villager named Denise fills a bucket with hazelnuts. She hangs the bucket at the end of the squirrel highway.

Some days squirrels wait in the trees for Denise to arrive.

Hazelnuts, chestnuts, and walnuts are the red squirrels' favorite foods.

belcanto
50 Boules de Graisse
avec filet
FABRIQUÉ EN FRANCE

The squirrels are happy to find the nuts. They eat some now. They take others away to bury in the ground. The squirrel plans to eat these nuts later. But sometimes they forget where they put the nuts! Those nuts often grow into new trees. This helps keep the forest healthy.

Some trees have special feeder boxes attached to them.

The Nutty Narrows Bridge

Dominique's squirrel bridge is not the only one. In Longview, Washington, a bridge called Nutty Narrows has been helping squirrels for almost 60 years. A man named Amos Peters got tired of seeing squirrels hit on the road. So Amos built a bridge over the road. His Nutty Narrows Bridge has been saving squirrels ever since.

This sculpture in Longview was built to honor Amos Peters.

LONGVIEW, WA.   MARCH 19, 1963
NUTTY NARROWS BRIDGE
Constructed by Amos J. Peters, Construction

Save the Squirrels!

People all over the world have built squirrel bridges. They want to help these creatures stay alive. It is because of people like Dominique, Laurent, Amos and their friends that squirrels can live long, healthy lives. And they will continue to help replant our forests.

Glossary

anchored: attached, held onto

donated: gave to someone
for free

extinct: no longer exists

pulleys: wheels with ropes around
them, used to lift heavy weight

Learn More in the Library

Einhorn, Kama. *Raccoon Rescue (True Tales of Rescue series)*. HMH Books for Young Readers, 2019.

Jane, Russ. *The Red Squirrel Book*. Graffeg Press, 2019.

Nicholls, Will. *On the Trail of Red Squirrels*. Wagtail Press, 1999.

About the Authors

Maxime Bonneau focuses his camera and his writing on social themes and animal stories. It was while scuba diving in 2009 that Max discovered his passion for photography. With his writing and photography, he hopes to help people discover the beauties of Nature, but also to raise awareness of environmental and social conditions. Max lives and works in Compiègne, France.

Joanne Mattern is the author of many books for children including the Core Content: ***Earth's Amazing Animals Series***. She loves writing about sports, all kinds of animals, and interesting people. Mattern lives in New York State with her family.